MAMA, DO YOU LOVE ME?

by Barbara M. Joosse

illustrated by Barbara Lavallee

Little, Brown and Company

Boston · Toronto · London

Mama, do you love me?

Yes I do,
Dear One.

How much?

I love you more
than the raven loves
his treasure,

more than the dog loves his tail,
more than the whale loves his spout.

How long?

I'll love you until
the umiak flies
into the darkness,
till the stars turn
to fish in the sky,
and the puffin howls at the moon.

Mama, what if I carried our eggs—
our ptarmigan eggs!—

and I tried to be careful,
and I tried to walk slowly,
but I fell
and the eggs broke?

Then I would be sorry.
But still,
I would love you.

What if I put salmon
in your parka,
  ermine in your mittens,
  and lemmings in
  your mukluks?

Then I would be angry.

What if I threw
water at our lamp?

Then, Dear One,
    I would be very angry.
    But still,
        I would love you.

What if I ran away?

Then I would be worried.

What if I stayed away and sang with the wolves
and slept in a cave?

Then, Dear One, I would be very sad.
But still, I would love you.

What if I turned into
a musk-ox?

Then I would be surprised.

What if I turned into a walrus?

Then I would
be surprised
and a bit scared.

What if I turned
into a polar bear,
and I was the
fiercest bear you ever saw

and I had sharp, shiny teeth,
and I chased you into your tent
and you cried?

Then I would be very surprised
and very scared.

But still,
inside the bear,
you would be you,
and I would love you.

I will love you,
forever and for always,
because you are
my Dear One.

Though often referred to as "Eskimos" (an Indian word), Eskimos call themselves Inuit (IN-oo-eet) which means "the people." (One Inuit person is called an Inuk.) There are many different Inuit nations, and each has its own language and traditions. Most Inuit live in the Arctic—the area around the North Pole. It is one of the coldest regions on earth. During the winter, there are months when the sun doesn't shine; in summer there are months when the sun never sets. Greenland, Northern Canada, parts of Russia, Scandinavia and Alaska are all part of the Arctic region.

The Inuit in this story live in the northern part of Alaska, where they have lived for more than 9,000 years. There are no cities in this part of Alaska. In fact, there are hardly any roads. This book shows the way Inuit lived many years ago. Now most Inuit live in a way that combines the old and the new.

Dog   Traditionally, the Inuit depended on dogs (known as huskies) to pull their sledges. Now, many Inuit use snowmobiles as well.

Ermine   This is the most widely used name for the short-tailed stoat. In the winter, its fur turns white—except for a black tip on its tail. This is when it is called an ermine.

Igloo   This is the Inuit word for "house." Because wood isn't available in many parts of the Arctic (there isn't enough sunlight for trees to grow), some Inuit build their homes out of snow. We call these homes igloos. The Alaska Inuit, however, generally only use snow igloos as temporary hunting shelters. They build winter dugouts of whale bone, driftwood, and earth. In the summer, they live in tents. Many Inuit now live in modern houses.

Lamp   The lamp in an Inuit home was never left untended because it was such a vital part of daily survival. It was used to heat the home, melt snow for drinking water, dry clothing, and cook food. Lamps were carved out of soft stone and filled with oil from whale blubber and a wick of dried moss.

Lemming   There are many of these mouse-like creatures in the Arctic. They live in tunnels beneath the earth and snow, where it is much warmer than above ground. In the winter, their coats turn from brown to white. They are the only rodent whose fur changes colour.

Masks   Inuit believed that the medicine man could talk to the spirits. To do that, he would wear a different mask for different ceremonies. Inuit artists still make masks today, but they are usually for decoration, not for ceremonial use.

Mitten   If an Inuk needs to rest, and he does not have shelter, he takes off his mittens and sits on them.

Mukluk   These Inuit boots are made with fur. Traditionally, they were lined with moss, but today they are lined with felt.

Musk-ox   Musk-oxen are prehistoric animals dating from the last Ice Age. Like cattle, they graze in small herds. In the Spring, they shed their winter under-fur, which is then gathered to make sweaters and other clothes.

Parka   This familiar hooded jacket was first worn in the Arctic. A woman's parka has extra room in the back for her baby.

Polar Bear   These are the largest of all bears. They live on huge islands of ice in the far north where they blend in with the white landscape. "Nanook" is its Inuit name. The polar bear is the most dangerous animal in the Arctic.

Ptarmigan   These birds are found all across Alaska. They are snow-white in the winter and they have feathered feet to protect them from the cold. They lay one egg every seven days and these eggs are a treasured food of the Inuit. There are three varieties of ptarmigan: the willow ptarmigan, the rock ptarmigan, and the white-tailed ptarmigan. The willow ptarmigan is the state bird of Alaska.

Puffin   These colourful birds are found on the west coast of Alaska. They live on the sea and on cliffs that rise from the sea. They are not very good flyers—their landings are so bumpy they can only land on water or soft grass. But they can "fly" very well underwater, where they use their wings as paddles. In the winter, their beaks change from bright orange to a duller greyish orange.

Ravens   Known in many places as crows, Inuit call these familiar birds ravens. Found in folktales throughout the world, ravens play a particularly important part in Inuit culture because Inuit believe that after death people return as ravens. It is considered bad luck to kill a raven. Ravens are the most common birds to be found all year round in the Arctic.

Salmon   A variety of salmon can be found in Alaska's streams and rivers. Inuit catch salmon in the summer. Then they're smoked, dried or frozen in the permafrost (the ground just beneath the surface, which stays frozen all year round) and saved for winter.

Umiak   These boats are made of whalebone covered with animal skins. They're used for travelling and to hunt whale. (A smaller, more commonly known version of this boat is a kayak.)

Walrus   These mammals live on pack ice (ice that's several feet thick and covers many miles), that floats in the Arctic Ocean. They have whiskers that they use to skim the ocean floor in search of food. They use their tusks to manoeuvre their young, to break ice, and to fight. Their family name, Odobenidae, means "those who walk with their teeth." Inuit use walrus hide to make fishing lines and boats. The meat is used as food.

Whale   Whales are mammals, not fish. Their blubber can be used as both food and fuel. The Inuit hunt whale in the summer, when the ice has broken up enough to move their umiaks through the water. Some whales common to the arctic region are: Belugas, Blue Whales, and Killer Whales. The whale in this book is a Bowhead.

Wolf   Wolves hunt together in packs, obeying a leader. They form close families and are gentle, playful parents to their young.